Written by Moira Butterfield

Illustrated by Rosalind Beardshaw

Designed by Lisa Sturley

This edition published by Parragon in 2011

Parragon
Queen Street House
4 Queen Street
Bath BA1 1HE, UK

ISBN 978-1-4454-3457-5

Printed in China

Smile
baby
smile

PaRragon

Bath · New York · Singapore · Hong Kong · Cologne · Delhi
Melbourne · Amsterdam · Johannesburg · Auckland · Shenzhen

The sun shone.
The birds flew.
The flowers grew.

But the baby...

The sister tried singing.

The brother tried swinging.

The mommy said **"Coo."**

The daddy said "**Boo!**"

But the baby...

cried!

The sister went clap, clap, giggle.

The brother made his fingers wiggle.

The mommy made
a shiny star.

The daddy drove around in the car.

But the baby...

The sister kissed
the baby's toes.

The brother kissed
the baby's nose.

The mommy hugged the baby tight.

The daddy kissed them
all good night.

Then the baby did a funny **burp**....

burp

...and then the baby...

...smiled!